MW01241614

Moments We Love

Poetry by

Balroop Singh

Copyright   2019 by Balroop Singh
balroop@rediffmail.com
https://balroop2013.wordpress.com

ISBN: 9798556995048

All rights reserved. No parts of this book
may be reproduced by any means: graphic,
electronic or mechanical, including
photocopying, recording, taping or by any
information retrieval system without the
written permission of the author except in
the case of brief quotations embodied in
critical reviews.

All the poems in this book are imaginative
but inspired from life.

Dedicated to my
grandchildren:

Athena, Elijah,

Rigby and Violet

who have given me myriads
of moments to cherish.

Preface

A brilliant poet may not color the tangible but rather unearth the hues of the intangible to coat specific dimensions to life. Balroop Singh masterfully spots the hues, decluttering them to seek particularity, taking us to the core of her dynamic worldview. *'Words just swirled around us, Eager to be spoken, Sitting on the tip of tongues, We were guessing, The stories that lay within'* is one of her call-outs to help unhide the potent of what we don't express.

Moments We Love is an enthralling and affecting spread of poems on a table where Balroop's polished menu commands that the cuisines of life be consumed gently, each breath be taken consciously, and the fleeting feels between the lines be mined timely.

While *'Breezy silence of your eyes, When they stirred skies'* points to the unimaginable possibilities of a heart with warmth, and *'Morning mist obscured my view, Chilly winds enveloped me, Yet the lure of unknown love'* romances us into the sweetness of longing, *'I pass by this* desolate path, *Receding foliage reminds me, Blossoms don't smile here*' singes our passivity to avoid a future of disquiet.

What oxygenates in the book for the reader is the author's uncompromising clarity that flows inward, and while it brims inside with rhythm and melody, we begin to make sense of what rushes outward, altering perspectives. And though the world that her words weave reflects our realities, she doesn't abandon us for her webs of hard truths—if maneuvered lovingly, have solutions within. '*A precursor of serenity, Glimmer glows within me, I abandoned your crutches.*'

When I was reading the book, I was constantly reminded of the likelihood that some of the poems might be autobiographical, impressing me since only a brave and intelligent writer could dish out the emotions like she did; only a compassionate writer could stand in the line of fire and yet smile, and yet be thoroughly objective for the benefit of the others.

Book after book that Balroop has penned, she has been unwaveringly consistent with her universal themes. And with **Moments**

We Love, she eloquently inspires us to believe in self and stand tall without fear; that our fear is indeed our solution. The impact of her verse is such that when I look at a peach and think that if peach were fear and its seed a solution, I can chew through the fruit—gently and consciously and through the heartbeats of resistance—to find my solution. Well, Balroop can unearth the hues of the seed without a single bite, which defines her writing.

Like she writes, *'Still holding the fragments? Still haunted by ghosts? Loosen that grip, Let the demons fly.'* Yes, I say. Eat your fear. After all, the solution is at the core and we can plant the seed to sprout more solutions.

— **Mahesh Nair**

Savor the Moments...

Moments of fragrant love that stand frozen in time, of dreams that dare not unfold, of passion that fleets by, of erratic joy that we meet at the crossroads of life; butterflies of time that add color to our dark moments to scare the demons away – I have gathered all of them in this book. Some of them whisper softly to create a magical aura while spring of life sings with them, trying to wipe silent tears. Mother Nature steps in with all her grandeur to breath quiet messages of tranquility.

Each poem would soothe your emotions with élan and add a dash of color to your life. Life – that doesn't halt for your sad moments; it just floats by. You just need to dive in to soak in myriads of moments to discover how they could ignite positive tones. All the poems in this collection are imaginary but inspired from people around me, some of whom chose to share their frustrations and tremors with me. My imaginative muse transformed them into poetry.

Memories and moments merge here
Today when I return to share

The glow of rainbows,
Embers of emotional entreaties
And smoldering debris.
© **Balroop Singh**

Contents:

SECTION: 1

Moments of Love:

SECTION: 2

Moments of Harmony:

Now I understand you!

SECTION: 3

Moments that make Life:

Wishes
Buried Dreams
Isolated Child
Keep that Smile
Awakening
My Muse Speaks...
Moments to Hold
I Hold my Dream
My Little Box
Literary Beetles
My Words
Rise Above Self
Waiting
Fortitude
Masks
Waiting for Peace
I Rise Today
New Beginnings
Summit
Don't Dwell On It! Really?
Did I change?
I Feel Most Like Me...
Only Memories Are Mine
My Mother
Ruins that Speak

No Turning Back
A New Horizon
A Touch
Mentors
Magic Of Reflections
Magical Moments
Celestial Path
I Know You
Eternal Wait
When I Go
The Last Smile

SECTION – 1

Moments of Love

Frozen in love
We stand together to clasp
Sublime serenity

♥

First love

Eyes brimming with dreams
An edgy threshold
A missed heartbeat
A craving within

First love is like
A cascading creek
Eager to rush
Unaware of pitfalls

Like a blooming bud
First love beams bright
Brings distinct delight
Lights up our life

Delicate like dewdrops
Donning tantalizing attire
Dauntless in its flight
Soars on the wings of whim.

Love Lingers

When first love was blooming
Its fragrance was confusing
Your mute messages
Difficult to decode but
Your efforts were amusing

Words just swirled around us
Eager to be spoken
Sitting on the tip of tongues
We were guessing
The stories that lay within

A thousand stars around us
Yet light eluding
Dreams dare not unfold
Fears shackled us
But love lingered

Swaying on the swing of desire
Inhaling the fragrance of fire
Fire that burns within
Carried far by the fiery passion
We craved to fly high.

Was It Love?

I know you loved me
But you didn't say it
The passion was missing.

You wanted me to fathom
But I didn't know
Love could be silent

I looked in your eyes
But couldn't see the spark
That ignites the flame

Was it fear or confusion?
Was it infatuation?
I was naïve

I didn't understand
Looking back, I can feel
The grace, the grandeur

That innocent love holds
Treading with poise
You kept testing the waters
And I swam away!

Love Yearnings

If you were wind
Would you blow softly?
Kissing my cheeks
Playing with my hair tenderly?

Would you boost my dreams
And carry them on your wings
To meet your charming friends
Drifting gently in the sky?

Would you fetch the fragrance
Of flowers each night
To fill our hours with ecstasy
Of embracing each other blissfully?

If you were rain
Would you drench me
With the deluge of your cascading fall
Inundating my urges?

Would you carry me along
As you flow into streams
Of desire, whetted by torrent
Of yearning of ages?

Would you promise
To hold me in your heart,
Ensconce me in your memories
And never forget me?

Magic Of Love

The feather we found on the ledge
Is as precious as you
Its color matches your blue eyes
Impelling me to plunge
Into their depth.

Its delicacy – a familiar touch
Like the magic of your hands
Stirring chords, rousing desire
Breathing a mesmerizing message –
Love is recalcitrant.

It dissolves doubts
Every rule does it flout
Fears melt when you delve deeper
To see its azure light
Follow the magic of love!

Eternal Love

Like soft flowers under our feet
Like lovely drops of first rain
Like moonlight soothing our eyes
Love tiptoes into our life

It carries us far into wilderness,
Its magic unfolds with trust
Its gentle caresses mesmerize
Its fragrance ferries amorous delight

Love is that exquisite emotion
Which remains deeply dormant
Till that irresistible urge beckons
And it becomes a force to reckon

Love ignites a fire within us
A fire of passion, of quest, of possession
It leads us into new adventures
It makes life so exhilarating

Love drowns dreary thoughts
It gives wings to our heart,
It transports us into another world
A world of blissful choice

True love keeps smiling in our eyes
Like a fountain that never dries
It instills hope, respect, patience
The journey of love is so elating.

Memories and Moments

Our favorite meeting place
Where we found solace
Love still blooms there
With fragrance and care

Breezy silence of your eyes
When they stirred skies
And our dreams took flight
Spring sang with delight

Clouds carried our joy far
Our love lighted by every star
Lingered languidly on our lips
When our hearts chose ellipse

Memories and moments merge here
Today when we return to share
Nuances of nature and love
That permeates this alcove

Your fragrance still abounds
Blends in the melodious sounds
Echoing its infinite power
In the grandeur of this bower.

Moments That Echo

Each moment is precious
We try to cage it within our heart
Where it perches in perfect rampart
Embalmed by memories.

Moments of love croon around us
Offering eternal passion that blinds
Drowning in the deluge of delusion
Validating ephemeral enchantment!

Moments of joy glisten on the sand of time
Fleeting away faster than dappling light
Peeping through the corridors of life
At the mercy of others' delight!

Woeful moments smile through strife
Each one stretching far and wide
Into every nerve and sinew
Sneering at our impertinent divide.

Each moment an experience in itself
We grow in its glow to wend and win
Divesting the ignorance of our thoughts
Solace echoing within!

When Love Whispers

We walked those woods
A thousand times
The silence; the symphonies
The shadows; the light

Lingering in the aura of love
Velvety sky watches
Stars shine brighter
With our whispers

Our love deeper than woods
Paces through night
Swaying with the breeze
Stilling my heart, singing lullabies.

Moments that Glow

Blissful moments of togetherness,
Soft reminders of love,
Add glow to the setting sun
When we walk toward horizon

Each moment magnifies our ecstasy,
Each moment a new dream,
Wafts around me
Mingles with your breath

Your breath brightens my passion,
Redefines my love,
I want to clasp these moments
To never let go.

Soaking Wet

Music could be heard all night
A soft rhythmic sound
Lulled me to sleep
As we snuggled into each other

I woke up with the same melody
It seemed too early
But eager to feel the cadence
That Glided down the leaves

I sat by my window,
Watching treetops
Swaying with the harmony
Of falling raindrops

Not a soul stirred
Not a bird flitted
The meandering path uphill
Bathed in romance

Hand in hand we walked up
Soaking wet in the glory
Of nostalgia
And eternal love.

Rift

Rift deep inside.
Drifting away into unknown self
I carry a smiling visage
With visions of drenched love

I pass by this desolate path
Receding foliage reminds me
Blossoms don't smile here
Stoic symphonies breathe within

Knowing well –
It started with a chink
A little opening to breathe
A little freedom of giving space

We just counted our flaws
And laughed together
When did it become a fissure?
Wide enough to devour us!

We lie trapped in darkness
In the shadows of stillness
Butterflies of hope are fluttering
With tears in silent eyes.

A Volcano

Days of distress simmered within
A volcano of
Love and hatred rumbled

Craters and chasms widened
Love got smothered
By sheaths of spite.

Demons exulted at alienation
Grudges deepened
Venom spewers smirked

Till lava flowed freely
Scalding happy onlookers
And manipulators.

Time traversed farther
To fill fissures of dissent
Peace and forgiveness triumphed.

Embracing silence
Fears receded,
Realms of rancor defeated.

Drifting Apart

Our love is losing its lustre
Like the setting sun
Slowly fading away
At the horizon

Surrounded by clouds
Of distress and doubt
Memories swirl around
Reminscent of romantic times

Circumstantial conflagrations
Encompass us
Stifling slowly
Snuffing life out

Expectations have perished
Clouds refuse to recede
Your eyes efface all hope
My faith is collapsing

Let's meet one more time
Before we drift apart
I want to re-live those moments
Of promising eternal love.

Superfluous

We've stood the test of time
Ever together, never alone

Weathering storms
Fighting strife
Dumped on the side,
We lie abandoned, alone.

Just like water
That flows
On a changed course
Leaving its residue behind.

Just like people
Who never look back
Once their purpose
Of using and abusing
Is done.

Just like path
That meanders
Through wilderness
Misleading new travelers.

Just like twilight
That is sheathed

By dark clouds
Hiding hues of sky.

Just like the stars
That shine unseen
When Sun makes them
Superfluous.

Remember Me?

I am the glow
That gleams between clouds
Forming rainbows

I am the rain
That falls slowly
Lingering on bare branches

I am the wind
That knocks at windows
To convey mystical messages

I am the sleet
That sits solemnly
Blinking at your attitude

I am that drop of nectar
You chose to mix
In the concoction called life.

Thaw

The warmth of walking beside you
Just like wrapping that old blanket
The wait for your cold arm
Yearning to reach me
That ear shattering peace
Eased by the doves above

Icy winds – a somber reminder
Of fragile emotional embankments
A laconic reply – a clear message
Yet those sunbeams
Dappling on the alienated path
Alluring us toward each other

Embers are alive within
Mist around the eyes is receding
As I could hear unspoken words
Echoing smoldering emotions
Which were buried
At the behest of hubris.

Drop the Debris

Still holding the fragments?
Still haunted by ghosts?
Loosen that grip
Let the demons fly
Choice lies with you

Open those windows wide
Let the golden glow permeate
Let the walls breathe
Before the big blaze

Life is much more than
Holding debris
Step outside where path begins
Where blossoms beam
To welcome you.

Conniver!

Can I ever forget?
Or dismiss that moment?
When you turned against me
When love lost its sheen

Your fiery face haunts me
The promises seem empty
I yearn to discern
The spells you could churn

The charm you executed
The bewitching words
That you diffused
To accomplish what I refused

I dwell here alone
Walls closing on
Sharpening my sword
Vowing to cut the cord

The quandary that binds us
Breaks tonight
As I escape this citadel
With a specious story to tell.

A Rising

Morning mist obscured my view
Chilly winds enveloped me
Yet the lure of unknown love
Stood with open arms

Beckoning to embrace all
All that was obscure!

Completely taken
By your entreaties
I walked into the winter
Of a new relationship.

Strange shivers warned me
A warm light guided me

Gentle reassurance
Steered me,
Out of
The dark corridors.

Glimmer

Is that your glimmer that is blinding me?
But I love my darkness
Into which you pushed me
I rejoice in my own domain now

A glacial glimmer froze me
When Time stood still
To lend empathy to my cause
To harmonize my thoughts

A precursor of serenity
Glimmer glows within me
I abandoned your crutches
When I embraced dark clouds

Wafting on those clouds
I can see beyond schism
A new world is alluring me
Beyond narrow boundaries and judgments.

Forbidden Love

A pearly beauty with emerald eyes
Too young to fathom fragrance of love
Fell for an artist who knew
How to admire her beauty
And win her despite his infidelity

Drifting into dreams of forbidden love,
Intoxicated by the jaunt of innocence,
Forgetting self to live within moments,
Hiding behind the mist of circumstances,
She flew on the clouds of glee

Merging into the golden glow
Of her master's fame
Never doubting his selfish love
She learned to live just for him
Dreams do come true!

Who Are You?

Once again dusk descended
Alone she sat in deep thought
One more gorge
That seemed to devour her

Love entered from the back door
Sat by her side and smiled
She couldn't recognize the stranger
So she asked: "Who are you?"

"You knew me at birth
You stretched your arms
For me, you cried
When I didn't embrace you

You waited for me each day
Trying to figure out the touch
Of those whose pretense
You could see through!

You wailed and wailed
But couldn't reach out to me
Till fears ensconced you,
Nurtured you with their fangs

You lost trust in me
Shoving me away each time

But I am an innate emotion
You can no longer detest me.

I would follow you now
In the meadows
In the woods
Smiling at your beauty

I would drag you out
From those dark corridors
To show
I am always around."

You And Me

Reflections reflect you and me
Together for ages yet apart
We stand here
Our thirst unquenched.

Visitors come and go
Admire our vicinity to each other
Some capture us on the canvas
Of their minds

Others stand by to share
Their most guarded thoughts
Their stories of lost love
The mystery of love that lasts.

Those who came in a canoe
And stood to admire
My gnarled limbs last year
Their laughter created ripples

Breaking your conceited calm
It revealed your cryptic cravings
Though I reach all out to hold you
Yet remain rooted in my zone.

A solitary life seems delightful
As mute connections speak
Of spiritual bliss we share
Breathing contentment.

Do You Remember?

Do you remember the days?
When we played with clouds
Rolled in colors,
Wore them around
Drenched and smiled
When we splayed colors at each other.

Do you remember?
The day we entered the book of life
The path we shared,
The incandescence ensnared
But the Milky Way
Guided us out of dark alleys.

Do you remember?
The milestones we met
The roars of laughter,
The deafening silence
The rivulets of rancor
That we crossed hand in hand.

Now remember to relinquish
All those colors of love,
The moments we revered
With the hope
We would be remembered fondly
When our book closes.

Aberrant Love

Whirlpools whetted at his feet
He stood tall and still,
Feet firmly entrenched but
Forlorn, just with his love

Demands escalated each day
Fire of love fumed and licked,
Legacy was the first offering
Money was perpetually poured

But the acerbic vixen
Who trapped him in her maze
Could never get satiated
She claimed all he had.

Smoldering emotions reeked of spite
Family values trampled to alienate
Usurped in the name of love
Love that sucked all!

A walled fortress – his abode
No less than a cage
That nobody could enter
Where pretense and love prevailed.

Cold cadavers strewn around
He refused to acknowledge guilt
An altruism awardee
How could he ever go wrong!

Images Of Love

Brooding eyes, blasé yet discreet
Discerning depth of dark images
Wriggling away from the light
That glows to glean truth

Unstated grievances creep out
When I look within
All of you crawl like worms
Some faces visibly distraught

The artist could see you
My illusionary veil couldn't shroud
Graphic secrets of thoughts
That groan under pictorial patterns

Onlookers may admire the art
Only I know the depth it conceals
Come and alleviate agonies
Shared stories satiate our emotions.

Love Returns

We have found
Those tiny hands we searched
Those little feet that follow us
Those big eyes that beckon
Those angelic smiles to reckon

We take pride in
New love that is cuddlier
New bonds that clasp us
Delightful moments that glow
Rivulets of respect that flow

Now we know
If it pervades our souls
Love returns in another form
Detachment is just an illusion
It unlocks the secrets of delusion

Let's not forget
Whatever you give comes back
Selfless and real love returns
Instill the value of love
Pour it in its purest form.

(Dedicated to my dearest grandchildren)

Love Is Weird...

If I were a bird
I would sing my sweetest song
To delight you all day long

If I were a flower
I would beam brighter at your gaze
To let your smiles blaze

If I were wind
I would sway your swing
Cheering you always

If I were a cloud
I would carry you along with me
To the horizon

If I were a butterfly
I would lend all my colors
To your lovely face

If I were a fairy
I would flutter around you with passion
Fulfilling all your desires

But I am only human
With limited capabilities
I can only write a poem for you.

(Dedicated to my dearest grandchildren)

Memories

Memories frozen in time
Are melting,
Stirring forgotten tears

Some emerge from
Dark crevices of heart,
Lurching weakly

The one I buried in books
Wriggled out,
Much enlightened

The one I submerged in stream
Of my thoughts
Is peeping out

The one I hid in the old house
Grew wings,
Craving for light.

Their grief was muted
Muffled callously,
Eager to share their gloomy journey

Memories gather this time
To mourn
In the arms of a poet.

Exulting at his expertise
Of offering solace – hollow
Hollow words of comfort!

My First Love

Poetry
is my first love
We wander
in the woods together
Hand in hand
we walk into wilderness
Sharing dreams
of land unseen
A world
that is really green
Where clouds
of kindness hover
With promises of peace.
Soaring on
the wings of words
Glistening
with a halcyon hope
Brightened by
enchanting thoughts
We recline on
the stratum of stars
Cooing gently
that they would be ours
One day
when elixir of love
Would caress
the feet of humanity.

Poetry

Poetry is hollow without emotions
Words just stare sans sheen
Soulful poetry tugs at heart
Wrapping words in sandpaper
Draping each emotion with electric élan

SECTION – 2

Moments of Harmony

Does Spring ever think of winter?
It blooms and smiles
So do we, intoxicated by life

Magical Fall

Nature nurtures my muse
Who sits by this waterfall
Soaking in the surreal wonders
Spellbound by heavenly hues

She treads on emerald rocks
To admire crimson leaves
She swings on bare branches
Her words swirl around with ease

Sometimes she flows with water
Drenching in moments of joy
Splashing to satiate her passion
Intoxicated by the magic of Fall

A cherished haunt, a lover's den
To which she returns each year
Seeking Mother Nature's veil
That absorbs anguish.

Transient Beauty

Draped in pristine white robes
I watched the adventurers
Gathering to admire my attire
And feel the fetish of my fire

Some stood frozen in awe
Angelic messages showering through
Blue, gray and silvery gear
Momentous moments to cheer!

Silvery sky soaked me entirely
With his wondrous frescoes
Painted with natural hues
To match my ensemble cues

I smile as they ski down the slopes
Once a year such fun ensues
Only when I change my dress
To gaze at some signs of progress

I blessed those who just stood there
To commemorate my transient beauty
Along with digital trophies they depart
Carrying exquisite memories in their heart.

("I" in this poem refers to snowy slopes of
Mother earth)

Summer Love

In awe I looked at you
And the shimmering dew
Bashful beauty allured green shade
In your welcome they all swayed

When you tiptoed in
To lend glow to our solitary town
Your sparkling light could make
Each moment of my day bright.

You illuminated our hearts
Just with your brighter days
The leaves and branches colluded
To bow to you in gratitude.

Coruscating lilies spoke to me
Roses beseeched my attention
Mute watchers warbled
Fluttering fervently around me

Fledglings are flying out now
Heralding the inevitable change
Birds breathe a message
Time has come to say goodbye.

Fall trots in complacently
Knocking off supremacy of the Sun
Leaves sing new melodies
But I crave for your celestial light.

Redwoods

Here I am on the tangible trail
Looking up in delight
Mesmerized by the height
Exhilarated by the light
Filtering through the circular canopies
Lost in the moment.

Here I stand merging in the trees
Awed by their grandeur
Dazzled by their magnificence
Startled by the decay
New shoots sprouting from
Dead trees, testifying their latent power.

Mother Nature smiles sweetly
As I stand, intimidated and
Intoxicated by the fragrance of flora
Flourishing amid ironic beauty
Of fire damaged trunks
Standing tall to tell their seminal story.

Time – a mute spectator
Watches wistfully, losing its hold
Connection with the world seems
insignificant
The haunting beauty returns in dreams
Transporting me to darker trails
You can never have enough of this delight.

I Dived In To Discover

This brook breathed a quiet message
Why do you write poems?
Write about people
Write about their whims
And their stings!
I nodded.

Yet I dived in to gather its colors
Divine blues and greens
Merging shadows smiled
In harmony with the breeze
And swaying trees
Gauging my nods.

Shadows know me well
I have walked with them
Far away into the sky and sea
Sinking and shining together
Swaying in all kinds of weather
Driving darkness away.

As the water mirror meandered
To unravel its beauty
Birds joined in to mesmerize
Green vibes permeated around
I was soaking wet with them
I knew why I was numb.

Chained

The wind whispered: "let's fly"
She looked around: "I can't."
"I'm like the lithe leaf
I can only flutter."

"I'm chained by circumstances
Tied to cliffs.
I no longer complain
I love my solitude."

Wind unleashed its power
Dismantled all doors of diffidence.
Despair flew with her
Self-created shackles dropped.

Clouds ceded their power
Birds beseeched with buoyance.
Horizon glimmered and
The bridge beckoned.

It was time to cross over
Into the realms of freedom
Beyond societal shams
Beyond walls of wanglers.

Watch the Magic...

Strokes of crimson herald the change
Ochre tries to meet at the edges,
With reverence I look around
At majestic branches almost bare.

Deep shadows dance around me
Wind and breeze compete to win.
Far away, at the horizon, gray scrambles
To steal some golden kisses.

A waterfall accentuates this beauty
And the valley resounds with a voice,
A familiar melody – melts all my angst
Now I know what allures me here.

Ferns flock like old friends
Blankets - that warm aching hearts,
Patterns of joy inked in green
Calm chaos that lay hidden.

That is the magic of a changing season
Just step out and watch the spectacle.
Mother Nature looks magnificent
In all her outfits.

Autumn Roses

Fall fails to touch them
As they toss their heads.
Changing colors of autumn
Stand apart to smile smugly.

The garden is littered with leaves
West wind sings a new song
And shakes some placid petals
They lean in to please her.

Dancing wistfully,
Resplendent in their glory
These two roses
Not ready to say goodbye.

Dreamland

Purple robes of Mother Nature
In sync with her dreams
How long has she yearned for them?
I stand spellbound.

Celebrations start at dawn
Only couples are invited
Royal robes flutter fragrance
Sun shies away.

A whisper rides on breeze:
Far away from the land of conflicts
Welcome to the domain of dreams
Love blooms here.

Skeptics – please stay away
Echoes of love might devour your designs
We hold harmony in our hearts
Tethered to respect for all.

Silvery Serenity

Drowning in watery wails
I try to clutch the waning light
My eyes wander in a wild pursuit
Knowing not what they want.

What is this weird place?
Silver glistens in the sky
Lending its sparkle to waves
Not a soul in sight.

Who dumped me here?
A wilderness of my dreams
At least I can breathe!
Hope shimmers amid dark dunes.

Barefoot I walk toward the horizon
I would carve my way
Out of apathy and derision
Desolation doesn't dissuade me.

Soaking in silvery serenity
I exult at my new world
All fetters fall apart
Traces of humanity linger.

Rooted by Love

In summer and spring
We sing together
In winter and rain
We huddle closer
Showcasing earthly bonding
Evoking messages of togetherness
Radiating timeless joy.

We run around
Spreading joy
Visitors stand by to admire
Our tentacles
Reaching out to gather light
Clasping moments of delight.

Love is not just growing together
It is weathering storms
Smiling through gales
Reaching out to each other
Making memories
That could be cherished.

New Friends

Today I am visiting my new friends
They hang and swing merrily
Always together, drifting drowsily
Their laughter attracts many

Today they revel
In the glory of meeting her,
Their bewitching beloved
Whose grace surpasses all!

Supple and breezy
Cool and warm
She is loved
In all her forms

Sometimes they chase her
When she enthralls them
With her winged speed
Shouting over high hills

They change their hues
From dark deep blue
To burnt orange and ochre
Till inky night swallows them

Lulled by her, they sleep
Till dawn
To spread their smiles
And play with colors again.

Stuck At Sunset

Orange Ocean around me
Shifting hues
Awestruck, I gaze speechless
Pink and purple ribbons
Hang around me
Graying at the edges.
Golden glare
Evoking vibes of celestial love
What a spectacle!
When a perfect artist –
Mother Nature
Painted the sky
And threw all her colors
At crawling cars
Heading home
Feeling blessed...
Stuck at Freeway!

Colors

The day sun descended
With all his fire
To dilute the heat
Even clouds couldn't peep.

I watched with a gasp
When an azure pool
Changed its color to gold,
Heat flew like splinters.

Mother earth endured all.
Breathing quiet messages,
Branches stoop to offer shade
Moments of harmony sway.

Now this pool knows magic
As it changes colors
Passion and serenity meet here
When moon lends its silvery glow.

Heavenly Hues

They stood spellbound
Emerald bridge beckoned
The beauty around surreal
Were they close?

Two rivers in sight
One was under the bridge
The other right in front
Touching the horizon

One was bluish green
Vast and variegated
Merged into twilight colors
Orange and ochre

More like a conflagration
That had descended
To ignite serene waters
With heavenly hues

Rooted to the edge
Watching the spectacle
They were entranced
By the beauty of Mother Nature!

Spring Melodies

Once again our green hands
Disseminate sheltered serenity
Once again our life inspires
The love of perpetual giving

Come join the celebrations
Revel in the glory of spring melodies
Soft sounds of new leaves
Merge in the song of bluebirds

Recline in the carousel of lovebirds
Glide with the breezy fragrance
Smile with the colorful sweet peas
Feel the magical breath of spring

This green bower beckons
Accentuating avenues of harmony
Shifting seasons beseech quietly
To keep the rhythm of nature alive.

A Lament of Mother Earth

Frozen in time
With amorphia of ages
I sat waiting for love
It did come at last!

They came in hordes
With shovels and hoes
To dig around me
And create a cover

I welcome them
But arrows pierce my soul
Dirt and deceit blind me
I crave for a new world

My faith in smithereens
My perceptions upbeat
Each storm whittling away
Gold of my sun

Internal injuries expand
Putrefying precious limbs
Blood flows through fissures
But freezes.

Silvery glow refuses to fade
Spring smiles at the horizon
Promising to alleviate affliction
And apathy of ages.

Now I Understand You!

Dear old vagabond: Time
I love you when you move slowly
And let me listen to my heart
To count moments of bliss
To sit by the brook for hours
Savoring soft sounds

I love you when you choose to sit down
Weaving priceless webs with me
Watching my fingers trying to hold you
And trust your magic
Of erasing emotional hurts
Of creating magical memories

Not that I didn't appreciate
When you ran ahead
And taught me to compete with you
Without any rules
Offering me the best benchmarks
Smiling at my whirlpools

Not that I detested your game
Of turning tables on me
Changing at will, ticking away
Robbing me of my dreams
Stealing my momentous moments
Impelling me to follow your schemes

Dear drifter: now I understand you
You are just a wave that gushes forth
Just a whiff of wind that passes by
Just a moment that slips away
Just a powerful tyrant
Obliterating all, whenever you want!

SECTION – 3

Moments that Make Life

Some moments glisten
But real life occurs elsewhere
Shrouded in shades

Wishes

Wishes waft freely
Warbling with the wind
Some are eager to soar
Others lurk by the door

Some gleam like dewdrops
Others bury themselves in sand
Some embrace and enamor
Others yearn to taste glamor

Vying with each other to be seen
In the relentless race of growth
Love and success meet and clash
Traversing together only to crash

The red wish pushes ahead
Forgetting its pernicious passion
That rides on the mighty waves
Whose latent power never saves

The white wish waits patiently
Smiling softly to herself
Watching your antics with zeal
Knowing well she would heal.

Buried Dreams

Unknown dreams tumble out
On dark and dreary nights
When windows are misty
Mind wants to unwind

Clouds come crashing down
My pen floats away
Words flounder around me
I watch with dismay

Songs of love and harmony
Slivers of memories
Clutch my hand
We stray away into oblivion

To discard wilted flowers
Fragrance frozen within
Dreams don't change life
It takes its own course

Waiting for the morning star
I lie bleary-eyed
To bury those dreams
One more time.

Isolated Child

She stood there
Transfixed to the wall
Hearing those words of censure
Wondering why she was accused
If tears refused to fall,
If pain didn't display,
If feelings froze within,
How could she
Pretend to grieve?
But her heart bled,
Tiny drops snuffing life out
When embers burnt within
Reducing her to ash
Never could she share
Even with the stars
How forlorn was her path!

Just the Magic

What is this ache?
To delve deep —
Be it forest or sea
Of emotions or aspirations

Or is it the ache
To soar, to reach the unknown
To mingle in the glory
Of colors casting their spell?

Or just the magic
That unfolds before us
Offering opportunities
Opening new portals?

Some aches never subside
We hold on to the magic of life —
A mirror, that reflects
Fragments we hold dear

An illusion that would breach,
Tossing up treasured moments,
Groping in the darkened realms
Trying to find new light.

Keep That Smile!

The strong and the mighty
Try to push you around
Whatever the weather
They don't want you together

"Why are you happy?"
"How could you...without me?"
I hold the power
How dare you flower?

Is it jealousy or arrogance?
Lack of love or loneliness?
Humility at their feet,
They trample you with conceit

Domineering seems to be their right
Insecurities weaken their hearts
Love vibes refuse to step-in,
Aggression is their sole weapon

Yet they fail to snatch smiles
Which build bridges across miles
Little houses are a haven of peace,
Offer you ethereal ease.

Awakening

"Wake up," nudged my muse
I grimaced,

And immersed myself
Deeper into the sea of
Self-judgment and censure
Self-scorn and regret

Abyss of anguish threatened
Torrential tears of rue throttled
Chaotic thoughts clamored
Till awakening dawned

Till I could hear the whispery
Anecdotes of my muse
To soothe my splitting headaches
Tales of fortified resilience

Through turrets of time
I could watch the remnants,
The fragrance that lingers
The glory that hangs around me

Velvety memories float,
Silvery sky beckons me
A glow shimmers through clouds
Speaking syllables of commiseration

Awakening angel descends
To shower life-lessons...
Life is more than dwelling in sorrow
Let it flow with finesse.

My Muse Speaks...

'Is life a bird?' I asked my muse
'Fleeting by unseen
Perching on treetops
But a moment.'

'No,' came the response
'It's a stream
Hurtling down with abandon
Dealing with boulders.'

'It's a flower
That lends fragrance
To all
But love only to one.'

'It's a magical fairy
That mesmerizes us
And lifts us to carry
Into her enchanted world.'

'It's a dream
That reclines on clouds
Adding an unknown charm
To soften sad moments.'

'It's a leaf
That smiles at the sun
And drifts away
Slowly with the wind.'

Moments To Hold

At the threshold of new life
Reflections gather and glimmer
Dreams bounce with joy
Mother Nature's sanity speaks

As she sits by the placid lake
Surrounded by hills
Marveling at the harmony
Of hues – blue green and azure

Melodies of nature calm her
Clouds collude to kiss the tops
Misty mountains smile
Mesmerized muse sings

Exquisite moments hold
Positive vibes of life
Connections seem eternal
Ah... the solace solitude brings!

Tranquility we yearn for
In the whirlwind called life
Both the journeys
Come with a price!

I Hold My Dream

In my hands
My own dream, my days
Defined by my reflections

In my hands
Moments when I flew
On the wings of imagination

Perching on dew
With caution, a little apprehensive
I hold my dream

Oh you can't even have
An iota of inkling
Of the rivulets of rapture
That flow within me!

My Little Box

Ensconced in that little box,
Sit my precious dreams
Hidden from the world
They may never see the light.

Lulled into calm corners,
They slipped into deep slumber
I admire their poise
Of holding their breath.

I dread opening the box,
Butterflies are eager to fly
I am guilty of smothering them
They are too dear to discard.

I push my way through
Deep valleys to rumbling clouds
Undeterred by lightning
Fervidly seeking success.

Life whispers through the mirror
I ignore its entreaties
Inebriation of youth is wearing off
Yet I clutch my little box.

Literary Beetles

Gold couldn't lure us
We are literary beetles
We walk at will, making our own trail.

Destinations don't hold us
We scatter words that shimmer
The sky is our canvas.

Our burrows are cavernous
We bury dreams in them
They reverberate ruefully.

We wait for wings
To excavate our aspirations
Of touching the horizon.

The path may be treacherous
Our feet may be feeble
Yet we walk undeterred
Impelled by each other's whisper.

My Words

My inkpot is empty
My words hang in the air
Yearning to communicate.

I stir my words in the teacup
Their warmth is wafting
Eager to touch you.

I try to carve them on your heart
They melt and mix in your blood
Losing their charm.

How will posterity read them?
I need new inkpots
My journal is wistful and forlorn.

My poetry has always regaled him
With zephyrs of words –
Words that whisper and warble.

Rise Above Self

If I follow the light
Will the mist fall behind
To reveal the esoteric belief
Of rising above self?

If I rise like the rolling tide
Will I glide and reach the sky
Without trudging through trajectory
That is strewn with sharks?

If I sideline these hypocrites
Will I survive in this world
That is placed on crutches
Staggering to balance progress?

If I shut my eyes to constant strife
Will the world heal itself
Teetering on the precipice of
Avarice, apathy and prejudice?

Waiting...

A part of me got lost
In darkness
I've been waiting
To identify it

Shadows of solace
Streaks of moonlight
Keep me awake
Heavy footsteps keep vigil

Endless night – a longing
Reminiscent of
A recurring dream
A haunting journey

With eagerness to emerge
Into an enlightened world
Abandoning attachment
Of this dark domain

Waiting for the whisper
Of stars, the warmth of
Eternal exuberance
A binding that is timeless.

Fortitude

Darkness thickens around me
I sit still as it creeps on me
Words freeze in my throat
I wait for my turncoat

Strange sounds scare me
As I muster my strength
Some light within me flickers
Fireflies inspire with their whispers

I try to decipher their message
The winding staircase beckons
But I sit rooted to ground
Demons of doubt hover around

A sudden wave wends my way
Whetting the desire to run
Pulling my feet with credence
I venture one more defense

Even if I crawl on four
Even if it hurts encore
I must try once more
And refuse to live a life I abhor.

Masks

I could hear the whisper
Which you didn't share
Wind couldn't carry it far
As I caught it.

I could discern the dislike
Dawdling in your words
A silent soliloquy lingering
Behind the blustering bastions

I wanted to scream
Speak! Why cant you speak
Let those words out!
Reveal your real face!

Pretensions peep through pores
Hiding behind masks
Can't conceal conceit
That percolates through.

Waiting for Peace

You could see her
Even on misty mornings
Waiting at the top of the hill
Melancholy figure, standing still

Oblivious of slander or censure
Immersed in her own beliefs
She moved up and down
Never could she see the town

People shook their head in distress
Counted her among the dead
How could she fall for the bait?
How long would she wait?

She knew that dawn so well
Coruscating rays welcomed them
Mist was nowhere to be seen
Could she ever forget the scene?

Promises of peace went awry
Hazy message stood before her
Yet hope lingered at the corners
Drifting away from the mourners.

I Rise Today

I have been lying low
I have been waiting,
Waiting for this moment
The right moment to leap out

It is now, I tell myself
'Togetherness' was the day -
"When they meet in wee hours,
Both the sources of light."

Eerie silence encompassed me
As I struggled out,
I tried to run toward light
A pull seized me

Shackles entrenched my feet,
Shadows seemed to smother
My spirits, but they soared
Higher than the skyscrapers

All cries froze on my lips.
In the grip of an unseen power,
As if my bones were melting
Rays were piercing like needles

Igniting my power
Of swallowing the darkness,
I spread my arms
To gather the diminishing light

The threshold of new life smiled
I rise today
To shake off the darkness
That has eclipsed mankind.

New Beginnings

Arid land, parched throats
But they walked on into wilderness
Inspired by the silvery light
Far away at the horizon

Hope could have propelled them
But a fire within was stronger
Stark realities around them
Death stared in empty eyes

Penury writ large on the faces
They had to make their own trail
Across the land they loved
Love could no longer ensnare

Darkness stirs new possibilities
Centaurus lights their path
A glorious new dawn waited
Far away near the horizon.

Summit

Fear watched in awe
Mist of doubt dissipated
As he climbed up dauntless
Talking only to his mettle

Friendly talk fell apart
At the speed he sustained
Daggers drawn at everyone
Knocking rivals down

Climbing upon carcasses
Swinging on subterfuge
Intoxicated by a vial of venom
In pursuit of self-glorification

Could a menacing sky dissuade him?
Could Earthly shackles restrain him?
Even woods and waterfalls
Couldn't persuade him

Not a moment of reflection
As summit beckoned him
He knew zenith was waiting
Just for him

Alone he stood, friendless,
Captive at the top of the world!
Contrite at his truimph
Success comes at a price!

Don't Dwell On It! Really?

When people offend you
Take you for granted
Don't respect your love
She says – don't dwell on it!

When they discriminate
Treat you like dirt
Walk all over you
She says – don't dwell on it!

When they belittle you
Mock at your kindness
Hurt your self-esteem
She says – don't dwell on it!

When Sun chooses windows
Leaving you in darkness
Depriving you of your right
Would you say – don't dwell on it?

When spring selects the privileged
And flowers don't smile at all of us
If butterflies visit only the best
Would you say – don't dwell on it?

If people had not dwelled
On atrocities heaped upon them
If they had not risen against

Discrimination and prejudices

If nobody had dwelled on
Equal rights for women
We'd still be living in dark ages
Repeating the refrain – 'don't dwell on it!'

Either she is too wise
Or I am indiscreet
Either way, I refuse to be dictated
Sensitivities need to be respected.

Did I Change?

When did this serenity step in?
Deep within me
Mixing in the blood
Blending with the bones.

Why are the waters so still?
Shimmering with revelation
Restoring fragmented breath
Calming earthly quest.

How did I change?
Accepting anguish inaudibly
Embracing forgiveness
As panacea for all troubles

Did I surrender?
When did I learn to be quiet?
So quiet in the face of falsehood
Or is it the poignant irony of life?

Life lessons beam around me
Skies have opened up
Proclaiming enigmatic epiphany
Exhorting me to agree with it.

Do I have a choice?

I Feel Most Like Me...

I feel most like me...
When I am home
When I can speak my heart out
Without thinking I'd be misconstrued
When I am surrounded by the people I love
The friends I can trust

I feel most like me
When I bask in the glory of my days
When I laugh like my grandkids
To add sparkle to my face
When happiness reflects in my eyes
My heart exults with pride

I feel most like me
When random memories make me smile
When rain drains away emotional dust
That gathers unawares
When my grandson hugs me tight
And whispers, "I love you."

I feel most like me
When my words flow like a stream
When my reflections are understood
And touch somebody's heart
When I have all the time in the world
To look at the stars

I feel most like me
When I am in my comfort zone
When I feel free to take decisions
That I know would be respected
When gratitude percolates within me
And peace pervades around

I feel most like me
When I listen to my inner voice
When I am unaffected by criticism
And stay calm in my heart
When I refuse to be manipulated
And can listen to divine within.

Only Memories Are Mine

I am thrilled beyond measure
But my eyes are brimming
Before me stands my home
The home that nurtured me.

A home that is whispering
A thousand stories
Of those carefree days
When stars were our confidantes.

With a flutter in my heart
I hurtle back in time
To hear orotund melodies
We sang louder than each other.

Emotions overwhelm me
As I step on the stairs
That gave a spring to my tiny feet
Yearning to open the gate.

Only memories are mine – not this house
Yet I could hear our lovely voices
That resounded in this house
Once upon a time.

My Mother

Who never wore armor
But is an epitome of strength
Who never wore a make-up
Yet her beauty is admirable

Who could digest rudeness
And forgive her perpetrators
Who could keep turmoil within
Alone, on dark dreary days

Who could rise from the abyss of grief
And sacrifice all her desires
Who possessed the mettle to push
The hungry wolves away!

Who could use any curse word
To keep you on the right track
Who forgot to smile
Yet could raise happy kids

Who has never said 'I love you'
But depth of her love is immeasurable
Who could knock off societal diktats
To nurture the dreams of her children.

No judgments could waver her confidence
No despair could drown her fortitude
Raging circumstances steeled her
Endowing her with incredible power.

She redefined the power of women
She lived through difficult times
Please don't criticize her
You can never fathom her strife.

Who are you to judge her?
You don't even know a moment,
Millions of which seared her soul
Yet she glistens brighter.

Ruins That Speak

I stand alone,
Reminiscing my glorious past
I rot but the decay dawdles.

Storms that I endured
Echo around me
Accentuating their power

Power that reeks
Of selfish goals
Will they ever fathom the futility?

Shrouded by deafening silence
Of ruin and devastation of
The land that nobody dares to tread

Dark moments cling to me,
Even waters run deep
Avoiding the valley.

Indifferent seasons secede,
Wind forgets to sing here,
Birds sit confounded.

Clouds pass by
Intimidated by the water
Whose colors run deep red.

Slime on stones has subsided
Trees recede to reflect
Muted tones ask but

Only sky that envelops me
Can tell the story
Of my collapse, of your debacle.

No Turning Back

Desolate path
Unknown goals
Yet she moved alone
Abandoning,
All that was hers.
Long wishful way
Full of stars –
The only motivation.

Lost choices,
No turning back
Dusk within,
A cloudless day
The weird way.
Confidence coerced her,
Twilight brightened
Her spirits.

Love withered away,
Mystic images
Besieged her
She didn't belong here,
She knew.
Crossing beckoned her
Yet some moments
Stood bare.

It was time
To gather those moments,
To break all barriers,
To cross over
Into an unknown land.
New horizon,
New hopes
Stood to welcome her.

A New Horizon

I didn't know this valley
The valley you pushed me into,
The valley that glimmers with hope,
That erases shadowy existence.

I owe you a special gratitude
I am glad I don't have to walk
Into your hollow world
Of pretense and glamor.

I have discovered a domain
Of buoyant blessings
I walk free now
A new horizon is beckoning.

The solace of open skies
Have melted all anger and anguish
The caverns that throttled me
Are far behind.

Opportunities are smiling
Love is all around me
Open arms of Mother Nature
Can descry and dispel despondency.

A Touch

I know I am not alone
Mother Nature holds my hand
Her elixir touches my feet
Her breeze ruffles my dreams

Her magical, dewy carpet
Carries calm whispers
Her lilting leaves remind me
Of songs that we sang together.

Yet I yearn for a touch
A touch that soothes
A touch of light that lingers
Wearing radiant robes of hope

Draped by dark clouds
With dreams wrapped in a shroud
I wait for your touch
That would infuse life into me.

Mentors

Light broke through the clouds
A grayish dawn danced
As dark clouds dissipated
Revealing a whisper of light

The warmth of celestial blessings
Could be felt within
A new path peeped
Through the wilderness of winter

Serenity of surroundings
Shielded our souls
When we walked toward freedom
Away from the hypocrisy of life

Life – that speaks in hyperboles
Life – that snatches away dreams
Life – that seems magical
And whispers words of wisdom

Paradoxical? But life is like that.

Magic Of Reflections

Meet this magic every day
Rein in your racing mind
Ask a question:
What's more important?

Meet those million thoughts
Immerse in their intensity
Sift the positive ones –
Those that bring happiness

Nurture those thoughts
That embrace pain
Seek your real self –
Self-reflection builds personalities

Lanes of life may be confusing
Yet traverse this maze with élan
A revisit may ravage your solitude
Some paths may harbor remorse

Reflections clear all cobwebs
Inspire intrinsic resilience
Magic unfolds
Unfettered by circumstances.

Magical Moments

Each morning we would rush out
To swim to the 'Angel Island'
Inhabited by colorful fairies
We wanted to live that belief.

Ah! The magic of moments
Enamored by the beauty around us
We made it our second home
Summer brought those blessings.

Showered with rose petals
We sailed into another world
A realm unknown to man
Where melodies of nature charmed.

Immersed in the poetry of water
We walked the magical path
Flowery beds beckoned us
We smiled sinking deep into reveries.

Intoxicated by the arabesque of fairies
We too twirled with joy
Friendship is a celestial gift –
Unequivocal and unparalleled.

Celestial Path

With the descent of dusk
A strange light dances
Between the trees
Fearlessly I follow the light
That grows brighter.

Far into unknown realms
A beauty beckons
Entwined with wisdom
Soaking my soul,
Warming my heart

Shadows seem to fade
Strange stillness envelops
An aura of calm creeps up
Self-awakening trundles along
Revealing celestial path.

I Know You!

I know you well
I know how you barge in
With your muffled face
To rob us of our happy days

I know your icy fingers are eagerly
Whetting their nails
To dig deeper into my veins
I have just one request:

Come softly...tiptoe into my room
Clasp me gently in my sleep
I know you are not so nice
But you can't be cruel to me twice.

Come when the sky is soft pink
I may not be awake to see
My soul would soak in the beauty
And leave this earth with good memories

My truce with you doesn't speak of love
You know I hate you
I have always hated you
Since you deprived me of my childhood.

Eternal Wait

Dwindling light merges into bare branches
Hours are crumbling into dust
A mute spectator of falling feathers
Waiting for change...

Hovering around the house of hope,
Believing in the triumph of dreams,
Comparing one state with another,
Waiting for eternity...

I don't want to be just a memory,
Just a nostalgic moment of love,
Just a shadow that glided by,
I wait for timeless connection.

I don't want to leave empty-handed.
Gilding love in a golden casket -
That is my perpetual desire
I wait for your momentous nod.

Together we float into another life
Together we open the golden casket
To discover the nuances of our love
Waiting for that celestial hour.

When I Go

Don't grieve over me when I go
I would be around you
In your laughter, in your mirth
In your reveries, in your recluse

I would live in your thoughts
My words would flutter merrily
To remind you
How transient is life!

My smiles would gleam
In the flowers of your garden
In the soft sounds of breeze
That would touch the trees

My memories would linger
Around you when you
Watch the clouds
And light that shimmers through

Look at the birds flying home
Let them calm you
With the thought –
Detachment is disconcerting
But true.

The Last Smile

This shady grove – my resting place
Lush green leaves – my lullabies
Fragrance of roses soothe me
Songs of nightingale regale me

But I can hear the sobbing too,
The moaning, the entreaties

Day after day he comes
To wake me up
To remind me of promises
Of eternal love

I yearn to break free
To rise and smile, one last time

To see the orange glow
Setting the clouds on fire
Many hues dance in between
As sun's last smile of the day fades.

✳✳✳✳✳✳

BY THE SAME AUTHOR:

Poetry: Sublime Shadows Of Life

Sublime Shadows Of Life is a book, which comments on life, its turbulent curves and relationships. It envisions people through the prism of poetry. I, you, he, we and they are universal symbols, which highlight the fact that happiness is not a destination but a chasm to bury agony, anguish, grief, distress and move on! No sea of solitude is so deep that it can drown us. Sometimes aspirations are trampled upon, the boulders of exploitation and discrimination may block your path but those who tread on undeterred are always successful.

Poetry: Emerging From Shadows

From darkness into light, from despair onto the wider ways of hope...life oscillates between sunshine and shadows. Emerging from shadows is a choice, which lies dormant, which can be gently inspired by self-talk. Each poem in this book banks on the hope of emerging stronger, saner, positive and resilient. Each poem in this book would talk to you, revealing layers of enclosed emotions. Each poem would divulge a secret path that could lead you into the world of poise and serenity.

When turbulences hit, when shadows of life darken, when they come like unseen robbers, with muffled exterior, when they threaten to shatter your dreams, it is better to break free rather than get sucked by the vortex of emotions.

Poetry: Timeless Echoes

Certain desires and thoughts remain within our heart, we can't express them, we wait for the right time, which never comes till they make inroads out of our most guarded fortresses to spill on to the pages of our choice. This collection is an echo of that love, which remained obscure, those yearnings that were suppressed, the regrets that we refuse to acknowledge. Many poems seem personal because they are written in first person but they have been inspired from the people around me – friends and acquaintances who shared their stories with me.

Some secrets have to remain buried
because they are ours
We do share them but only with the stars

The tears that guarded them were as
precious as flowers
Soothing like balm on festering scars.

While there are no boxes for grief and joy,
some persons in our life are more closely
associated with these emotions. Their
separation shatters us, their memories
echo, we grieve but life does not stagnate
for anyone...it is more like a river that flows
despite the boulders. When imagination
and inspiration tries to offer solace, poetry
that you are about to read springs forth.

When Success Eludes Us...

Success! The magic word that defines our
dreams! The potion that intoxicates! The
path that seems so tempting, so inspiring
yet so challenging! The chase that is
ceaseless, exasperating at times but
enlivens our lives!

Emotional Truths Of Relationships

Can we stop the flow and speed of
emotions? Can we learn from their
radiance, their cheerful bounce, their twists

and twirls? This book unravels their depth and resilience in handling the stormy weather, which is knitted into the fabric of all our relationships.

We look around and feel – 'Nothing is perfect'... dreams get shattered, hopes are belied, aspirations delude and the opportunities elude us. The clouds have the power to conceal the sunshine and our radiance fails to ignite positive thoughts. This book will guide you how you can keep pace with embellishing your thoughts and channelize your emotions, which can be trained to veer into a positive direction.

Read FREE with Kindle Unlimited

Allow Yourself To Be A Better Person

Do you think you are a good person? Would you like to meet your better self? Welcome to the vast vistas that this book unravels before you by highlighting the shaded areas that could never get your attention.

Enhancement of personality is a long process, which starts only when we acknowledge the need for it. Often we detest looking at our imperfections and if somebody is professionally successful, the thought doesn't even strike.

This book enlightens you about the goodness, which lies dormant within us till we make an effort to explore it. It exhorts you to introspect and accept natural human failings. It guides you towards the metamorphosis that could make you an endearing personality.

Buy from Amazon.com:

goo.gl/X1NEFf

Visit my Amazon author page.

ABOUT THE AUTHOR

Balroop Singh, a former teacher and an educationalist always had a passion for writing. She is a poet, a creative non-fiction writer, a relaxed blogger and a doting grandma. She writes about people, emotions and relationships. Her poetry highlights the fact that happiness is not a destination but a chasm to bury agony, anguish, grief, distress and move on! No sea of solitude is so deep that it can drown us. Sometimes aspirations are trampled upon, the boulders of exploitation and discrimination may block your path but those who tread on undeterred are always successful.

When turbulences hit, when shadows of life darken, when they come like unseen robbers, with muffled exterior, when they threaten to shatter your dreams, it is better to break free rather than get sucked by the vortex of emotions.

A self-published author, she is the poet of **_Sublime Shadows of Life_ , Emerging From Shadows**, and **Timeless Echoes,** widely acclaimed poetry books. She has also written **When Success Eludes, Emotional Truths Of Relationships Read FREE with Kindle Unlimited** and **Allow Yourself to be a Better Person.**

Balroop Singh has always lived through her heart. She is a great nature lover; she loves to watch birds flying home. The sunsets allure her with their varied hues that they lend to the sky. She can spend endless hours listening to the rustling leaves and the sound of waterfalls. The moonlight streaming through her garden, the flowers, the meadows, the butterflies cast a spell on her. She lives in San Ramon, California.

Made in the USA
Middletown, DE
18 September 2022

10662642R00070